The Adventures of Zelda: Pug and Peach

The Adventures of Zelda: Pug and Peach

Kristen Otte

The Adventures of Zelda: Pug and Peach

First Print Edition: 2014

Editor: Candace Johnson
Cover Design: Michael McFarland

ISBN: 1500710539
ISBN-13: 978-1500710538

This book is dedicated to Peach Doodle. You earned a chance for the spotlight.

Table of Contents

Chapter 1
The Mouth Game

I jump on Lucy's bed and curl up under the covers with her for the night. I close my eyes and let the exhaustion take over. My pug body is tired after a long day of playing and chasing my brand new sister. My sister is my Christmas gift. She was the best gift ever—making me the happiest pug on the planet. She is a Boston terrier, and her name is Peach.

Peach is a little bigger than I am, with tall, pointy ears, droopy lips, and a pug-like smashed face. Peach doesn't have nearly the number of wrinkles I do. She is dark, brindled-brown with patches of white, including a white stripe down her head to her nose, and a small peach spot on her nose. I think that's why she is named Peach.

1

Although she is a good-looking dog, Peach is not as pretty as me, especially since she doesn't have a curly tail. Her tail is short and a bit crooked. Honestly, I don't really care what she looks like; I am just excited to have a canine friend.

When I open my eyes the next day, light shines through the window, and the spot next to me is empty. Lucy is awake already. I stand and stretch—my body isn't used to all this exercise during the cold season. I hear movement downstairs as I go through my morning round of sneezes.

My family is gathered in the living room and eating breakfast. I see Peach nestled in a spot between Lucy and Hannah on the couch. Lucy is laughing as Peach repeatedly licks Lucy's face. I feel a pang of envy rip through me, but I ignore it and walk into the kitchen.

I smell bacon!

Nate is cooking in the kitchen, so I sit patiently next to him. If I stay calm, I am sure he will give me a piece of bacon. But it is so hard to remain calm when bacon is at stake. I sit and stare. I can't see the bacon, but the smell is overpowering.

Ruff. Ruff.

"Zelda, quiet," Nate says. I sit again. I didn't mean to bark, but I couldn't help it. Peach wanders into the kitchen.

"Hi, Peach," Nate says. "Do you want some bacon?" Peach trots over to Nate and starts leaping into the air.

She is springy!

"I think that means yes," Nate says, laughing. I inch closer to him. He better not forget about me. Nate grabs a piece of bacon. I do my best sit and stare at Nate with my bulgy, brown eyes.

"Good sit, Zelda," he says. "Peach, can you sit?" Peach continues to leap for the bacon while I wait patiently like the model pug that I am.

"No, Peach," he says and tries to get Peach to sit.

How long will I have to wait?

Finally, Peach sits, and Nate gives her a piece of the bacon.

"Good girl, Zelda," he says and gives me the remaining bacon. I scarf it up in a second.

"Okay, that's it for now. You're free," he says. I walk to the living room. Peach follows.

I find a comfortable spot on the couch next to Lucy. Peach jumps onto the couch and squeezes into the spot next to me. I look at her, and she nips at my face in a playful manner. I bite back, aiming for her mouth, but she shifts out of the way. I try again; this time she opens her mouth as mine approaches. We lock mouths, attempting to maneuver our mouths over top each other's.

We shift and squirm as the game continues, trying to get an advantage. Peach ends up upside down on Ben's lap. I jump on top of Peach, confident that I have her mouth cornered.

"Mom, what's happening?" Ben asks. I snap at Peach, but she dodges to the right. I pause for a moment to listen.

"They are playing, don't worry about it," Hannah says.

Oh, good. Hannah understands.

While I am distracted, Peach nips for my neck. I jerk backward just in time.

"They seem like they are trying to hurt each other," Ben says.

"No, this is how dogs play. If they were trying to hurt each other, you would know," Hannah says. "Although this is a funny game they are playing." I go in for the final bite.

I have her mouth!

"It kind of seems like they are trying to figure out whose mouth is bigger," Ben says. Hannah laughs.

"It does," Hannah responds.

I have Peach's mouth for only seconds before she wiggles her way out of the hold. But the moment of victory supercharges me. I leap off the couch and sprint around the coffee table, into the dining room, sliding as I go, and back to the living room. I jump to the couch and give Peach a quick nip, urging her to follow my next move. I leap again, but this time I run up the stairs and away from the slippery floor. I hear thumps behind me, and I know Peach is following. She catches up to me quickly, and I run under Lucy's bed. She's unable to fit, so she stops and barks at me. I lie on the floor panting for a few minutes. Peach keeps barking.

"What's going on up here?" Nate asks. He walks into the room. Peach stands on her hind legs and licks his hand. I crawl out from the bed.

"Oh, hi, Zelda. Come on, let's go downstairs," he says. We follow him downstairs to the living room. I see an open blanket.

"It looks like they are done playing the 'Whose Mouth Is Bigger' game," Ben says.

For now, but we will play again.

Chapter 2
Good Night, Peach

The rest of the day is a blur of games, chases, and sprints throughout the house. When the darkness comes, I am ready for a long night of sleep. I walk upstairs, leaving Peach and my family behind. I jump onto Lucy's bed. She isn't in bed yet, but I don't care. I plop onto the pillow and close my eyes.

"Okay, Lucy, time for you to go to bed," Hannah says. I open one of my eyes in time to see Lucy's hand coming for me. She picks me up and moves me to the side to claim her pillow.

"Hi, Zelda," she whispers. I gently lick her face. She covers me with a blanket before Hannah tucks her into bed.

"Mom, where is Peach going to sleep?" she asks.

"Peach is sleeping in the kitchen again tonight."

"Why?"

"In case she has to go to the bathroom in the middle of the night. She is still adjusting to her new home."

"Why can't she sleep with us?" Lucy asks. "She would be happier here than all alone."

With us? I don't want to share this bed and my Lucy-cuddles with Peach!

"I don't know if that's a good idea, Lucy. What if she has to go to the bathroom, and you don't wake up?"

"Please, Mom. I will wake up and take her out. And I bet Zelda wants to sleep with her new sister," Lucy says.

No, I don't!

Hannah remains silent. I raise my head and look at her trying to figure out how to convey my opinion on the matter. If only they could read my eyes and wrinkles like Peach does.

"Please," Lucy says again.

"Fine, okay," Hannah says.

"Yay!" Lucy shouts and rushes out of bed, flailing the blankets onto me. "Let's go get Peach!"

"Settle down, Lucy, it's still bedtime," Hannah mumbles as she follows Lucy out of the room.

I crawl out of the mound of blankets and find a comfortable spot at the head of the bed next to the pillow. Moments later Lucy, Hannah, and Peach return. Lucy finds her place under the covers again. Hannah picks up Peach and places her next to Lucy's feet. I relax, knowing my prime real estate next to Lucy is secure. Hannah says good night, and the darkness engulfs the room.

I jerk awake to a loud noise.

ONNNKSHHHHOOO.

Whatever is making that sound interrupted my squirrel dream. I had almost caught up to it!

ONNNKSHHHHOOO.

Yikes, that is loud. I am definitely not sleeping anymore.

ONNNKSHHHHOOO.

The sound is coming from the end of the bed. I tiptoe so I don't wake Lucy. Peach's smell overtakes my nostrils.

ONNNKSHHHHOOO.

I can't believe I didn't remember Peach was sleeping with us. She snores louder than I do! Although I don't really know how loud I snore, but it can't be this loud. I gently nudge Peach with my paw. She stirs; the snoring stops. I wander back to my spot.

Before I close my eyes, the snoring returns. I must not have woken her. I walk back and nudge Peach with my head.

Grrrr.

Her growl is halfhearted—she is definitely not completely conscious. I nudge again. This time she opens her eyes and gazes into mine. Then the tongue comes in a laser quick fashion, attacking my forehead before I can move. After she gets in one lick, I back away out of tongue range. She nestles back into her spot; I lie with Lucy's head on the pillow.

ONNNKSHHHHOOO.

Oh, man.

I squirm my way under the covers to escape the noise. I find a spot and nuzzle up to Lucy, but I still hear Peach. I can't escape it. I close my eyes and try to remember the dream I was having. I think about squirrels and my old friend Squeaks. My eyes feel so heavy.

ONNNKSHHHHOOO.

I keep my eyes closed and think about bacon and steak. I can almost smell it.

ONNNKSHHHHOOO.

I give up. I can't sleep with all the racket. I get out of bed and wander down the stairs to my blanket on the couch in the living room. The room is a bit chilly, but it's quiet. I fall asleep.

The next evening I claim my spot in Lucy's bed near the pillow. Peach follows me into the bedroom. She waits on the floor, unsure if she should jump on the bed. I am hopeful the loud snoring was a fluke. After a few minutes of staring, Peach makes the leap onto the bed. Her leap is more graceful than mine. One of these days, she needs to teach me how to jump like she does.

Peach sits in the middle of the bed, unsure about what to do. Lucy arrives and moves Peach to the foot of the bed again. Hannah and Nate say good night to all of us, and the darkness comes. I fall asleep.

When I wake up, Peach is lying next to me. I have no recollection of her arrival, and magically, she isn't snoring. Her warm body does feel good in this cold, but she squeezed her way between Lucy and me and stole my spot. I have no idea how she did it. I paw at her, but she is sound asleep. I don't see how I can move her. Frustrated, I rise and move to the end of the bed where I have space to stretch my paws.

ONNNKSHHHHOOO.

The snoring is back. I walk to the top of the bed. Peach is now sprawled across the pillow and the blankets.

ONNNKSHHHHOOO.

I am not sleeping here. I go downstairs to my new bed on the couch.

I sleep downstairs for the next few nights. I am comfortable, but I miss my cuddles with Lucy. When I wake up shivering one night, I decide it's time to reclaim my bed.

Long before Lucy goes to bed, I stake my claim by lying on Lucy's bed. When I hear footsteps coming up the stairs, I know it is bedtime. I smell Peach trailing behind Lucy, and I hunker down.

"Hi, Zelda," Lucy says, walking into the room. "Are you going to sleep with us tonight? I miss cuddling with you. You are so soft." Lucy gets into the bed next to me and pets me. Peach jumps onto the bed and tries to squirm her way between Lucy and me.

"Oh, hi, Peach," Lucy says, letting Peach squeeze in between us. I look at Lucy. She is smiling and laughing as Peach licks her face. I walk to the other side of Lucy, away from Peach. I curl up in a ball of pug fur next to her.

ONNNKSHHHHOOO.

Peach's loud snores awaken me, but her snores are coming from the foot of the bed. I get up, fumbling through the dark. *My spot is open!* I snuggle with Lucy and close my eyes. Peach is still snoring, but I am so tired that I barely hear her.

"Shhh, Peach is still sleeping," says Lucy. My eyes remain closed, but I listen carefully. Lucy's small fingers pet my forehead and back. The bed stirs, and I feel her getting out of bed. I hear the shaking of Peach's ears and collar from the other end of the bed. When I open my eyes, I am shocked to see light shining through the window. I slept through the night!

Peach wanders over to me and licks my face. I hate when she does that, but for some reason I let it happen. Then she nestles with me. Her body warms mine, and before I realize it, we drift to sleep again.

Chapter 3
The First Walk

The next few nights, I wake up less and less to the terrible snoring noise. Peach and I rotate our sleeping spots on the bed. Some nights I am next to Lucy. Other nights I am at the foot of the bed. I miss sleeping wherever I want, but this will have to do.

Today Peach and I are relaxing on the living room couch while the family paces throughout the house. I am daydreaming about treats when I see Nate put on his walking shoes. I perk up and watch him closely. He grabs the harnesses and leashes from the shelf.

It's time for a walk!

I jump up and sprint to him. I run in circles around Nate in excitement. I haven't been on a walk in forever because of the cold, white stuff. I don't think Peach has even gone on a walk yet!

Ben starts tying his shoes, and Peach joins us. She looks into my eyes, and I tell her we are going on a walk—the best thing ever. She is clueless about walks.

"Okay, okay," Nate says. "Zelda, chill out. I need to get your harness on you. Ben, you get Peach." I run another two laps before I allow Nate to harness me. My harness is blue. Peach is wearing a matching pink one.

"Okay, let's go!" Nate says. The four of us walk outside. The coldness hits my nostrils, and I sneeze four times before we get out of the driveway. Peach is hesitant, waiting by the door. I bark, telling her to follow us.

The white stuff is piled high, but the sidewalk is clear. I don't want to get lost in the snow, so I stay on the sidewalk. Ben and I lead the way. I hear Peach coming toward me from behind. Before I realize what is happening, Peach is jumping at me and biting for my neck. My instincts kick in, and I bite back. We tumble into the snow.

"Zelda, Peach, no," Nate says, pulling us apart.

I look at Peach. She thought it was playtime, but we have all this ground to sniff and explore.

We move forward, sniffing for clues of nearby dogs or squirrels. When we hit the intersection at the end of our street, I pull Ben to the right—our usual path.

"Which way, Dad?" Ben asks.

I lunge again, but Ben holds his ground. I stop and wait. Peach is trying to take us left. I glare at her. She goes left, ignoring me.

Doesn't she know I am a pug? I am not giving in.

I lunge right, dragging Ben with me.

"Zelda wants us to go this way," Ben says.

"Okay, that's fine. C'mon Peach, this way," Nate says.

Good call, Nate. I knew I liked you.

Peach turns and trots toward us, listening to Nate but not me. When she catches up to me, she takes a flying leap. I meet her on my hind legs and nip at her ears before I run as far away from her as my leash will allow. She whimpers, trying to get me to play with her, but I am busy sniffing for dogs and squirrels.

I amble forward, keeping my nose on high alert for an intriguing smell. Winter walks can be a bummer. Many of the animals are in hiding, and the white stuff mutes the smell. Plus it's hard to walk in the white stuff. The snow rises to my chest in many areas. I hear Peach approach me again, but this time something is different. I look to see that she is trembling with every step—Peach is freezing.

I could keep going for another hour around the neighborhood since I have thicker (and softer) fur than Peach. But I pick up the pace when I look into her sad eyes. When we are in sight of our home, Peach sprints for the door. I follow at a nice trot. When I cross through the front door, the warm air hits my wrinkles. It does feel good.

Peach meets me at the door and licks my face. After my harness is off me, Peach brings me the owl. I know she is thanking me for getting us home quickly. But today's walk has me wondering about the future. Maybe having a sister will change my life more than I imagined.

Chapter 4
The Toy Thief

Peach and I warm up under the blankets on the couch. Lucy takes turns petting us and giving kisses. After a few minutes, I slip out of the blanket and find a ball. I bring it to Lucy, and she throws it across the room. I grab the ball and bring it to Lucy. When she tries to grab the ball from me, I turn away and jump onto the floor. She chases me around the coffee table. When she finally catches me, I give up the ball. She throws the ball across the room again. I run to it, but Peach joins the fun. Peach slides into the ball and grabs it with her mouth. She runs back to Lucy.

After several rounds of ball with Peach and Lucy, I take a break on the couch. Lucy joins me on the couch, but Peach does not. Peach brings the ball over to a dog bed on the floor. She places the ball in the dog bed, turns around, and finds one of my owls. She takes the owl over to the dog bed. Next, she finds a blue Nylabone, and after a few minutes, all the toys in the living room are gathered in the bed. She returns to the bed, picks up one of the blue Nylabones, and plops down, surrounded by all the toys she collected. It is a strange sight.

"Mom," Lucy shouts. "Look what Peach did."

Hannah walks into the room.

"Peach has all the toys," Lucy says.

"I see that. Did you do that?" Hannah asks with a smile.

"No! Peach did that!"

"Huh. I guess she really likes toys." Hannah turns and walks back to the kitchen.

As I watch Peach chew on a Nylabone, the desire to chew burns inside. I see a second blue Nylabone sitting beside Peach. I jump down and go for the bone.

Rarrrf!

Peach barks and lunges at me, but I use my stealth pug powers to grab the Nylabone and get away. I guess she doesn't feel like sharing today.

I return to my spot on the couch and start chewing. The bone feels so good on my back teeth—the only teeth I have left besides the two front snaggleteeth. As I chew, I watch Peach chew her bone. Curiosity overtakes me. I get up and approach her slowly. When I am within one pug step, she stops chewing and looks at me. I take a half-pug-step forward. She starts growling.

That's not cool!

I step back. After a minute, she starts chewing again. I take a step forward.

Grrrrr.

I return to the couch. She won't look at me, so I don't know why she is upset. Maybe she doesn't want me ruining all of her hard toy-collecting work.

Yeah, that has to be it.

A few hours later, the toy collection is scattered throughout the house again, and Peach is acting like her normal, playful self. I am ready for another play session, so I find the squeakiest toy—the owl. I bring it to Peach, squeaking it as much as my pug mouth can. She takes the bait and charges for the owl in my mouth. I do a quick 180 and run the other way. The chase is on!

Peach is quick, but I can corner better than she can. I use that to my advantage by making quick turns and using my body to shield me from her attacks. But she catches on to my game, reverses course, and tackles me. She grabs the other side of the owl, and we play tug of war. I am losing my grip; I let it go. I don't want to lose any more teeth!

She runs the opposite direction and lies on the floor. I follow her. Peach doesn't even bother moving when I approach.

Grrrrrr.

Not again!

I back away and find a squeaky duck across the room. I am busy testing its squeaker when I feel Peach approaching. She swoops in and grabs hold of the duck. She shakes it, and I let loose. She runs away with the duck and finds a spot on the floor to chew it. When I approach, the growl returns.

She looks at me and tells me she doesn't want to play anymore. I back off. Bummed, I get some water and head upstairs to see what Ben is doing.

The next day I awake with Peach cuddled next to me. Today is a new day, and I am sure we will be back to normal. We all have bad days here and there, even pugs!

After our morning romp in the backyard and the mid-morning nap, I am ready to start my day. I go on a blue-Nylabone hunt. I find one pretty quickly, but I know a bigger one exists in the house somewhere. I find it upstairs under Lucy's bed. I have no idea how the bone got there, but I grab it and take it downstairs. I start chewing. The feeling on my teeth entrances me. I am in the bone zone. I barely notice Peach approaching me. I figure she wants to lie next to me, so I don't pay attention.

It happens in an instant. Her big head darts to the bone, and she secures it in her mouth. She lies down in the opposite direction with her butt and her crooked tail by my head. She starts chewing.

I am stunned. She stole my bone while I was in the bone zone! No pug would ever do that to another pug. But she surely isn't a pug.

I stomp over and stand next to her. She ignores me. I reach for the bone.

GRRRRRR.

What? There is no way she is getting away with this.

I try again, but she growls. I know I am quick enough to grab the bone and go, but maybe I don't want to do that. I can't read Peach. She isn't making sense, and I don't want her to be mad at me. Plus her mouth is bigger than mine.

I need a plan.

After a few hours of careful thought and spying, plus a few naps, I still have no idea how to solve this problem. My only plan is to improvise, and that doesn't sound like a good plan.

The dark has come for the day, but the family is awake and gathered in the living room. Peach and I are hanging out on the couch with Hannah and Nate. I think having the family around will work to my advantage, so I grab a blue Nylabone and start chewing.

Soon enough, I feel Peach approaching. She is going to steal the Nylabone again. I can sense it.

Should I let her?

Peach lunges for the bone, but across the room is another blue Nylabone, so I let her take my bone. If Peach sees we both can have bones or toys, maybe she won't want to steal mine all the time. I trot to the other one, grab it, and lie next to her. We both chew happily for a few minutes, which allows me to believe I have solved the mystery.

After a peaceful stretch of double chewing, Peach looks over at me. Her eyes have a hunger in them. She tells me to give her the bone.

Uh oh.

She casually scoots toward me. When she is within reach, she grabs my Nylabone, leaving hers behind. She starts chewing. I get up and grab the one she left behind on the floor. She is so busy chewing that she doesn't notice. I take it and sit on the couch.

While I chew on my bone, I realize something. Peach is a toy thief. I need to adapt, otherwise I will never get another toy. But since we both are chewing on bones, I know I am clever enough to survive with a toy thief.

Chapter 5
The Polar Vortex

The next few days pass without a major toy or bone incident. We have a few disagreements over bones and balls, but we manage to work it out. The mouth game remains one of our favorites, especially since we haven't been outside much. The white stuff continues to stack in the backyard. Nate keeps a path shoveled for us, but the snow outside the path is higher than my head. Occasionally I will trek into the uncharted territory if I'm on a squirrel- or dog-scent trail. But most of the time Peach and I stay on the path.

This morning Nate and Hannah put on our hoodies. I start running in circles, expecting a walk since we only wear our hoodies for a walk in the snow. Nate bundles up with more clothes than I have ever seen him wear. He walks to the back door, and I chase after him, confused as to why we are going out the back door instead of the front. When he opens the door, a terrible, freezing wind hits my wrinkles. I tremble and follow him outside.

"Peach, let's go," Nate says. She is standing at the door, not moving. "C'mon, time to go outside." Peach looks at Nate like he is nuts. She has no interest in going outside. Nate walks back into the doorway, lifts Peach outside, and shuts the door.

"Okay, c'mon," he says, walking on the path to the back.

I run in front of him and sprint to the fence—my regular route. When I reach the fence, I am winded. The frigid air hurts my lungs when I breathe. My ears are frozen to my head, and my paws are beginning to ache from the contact with the very cold air. It's never been this cold before. I turn and look at Peach. She is waiting by the door, trembling. I need to hurry up. I find the spot, quickly do my business, and sprint to the house.

After a few sprints, I start goose honking. It's so hard to breathe out here. When I finally catch my breath, I move slowly to help my lungs process the very cold air. As I walk to the door, one of my back paws starts aching. My toes feel frozen together. I lift the paw and continue the trek on three legs. It's not ideal, but I can manage. As I hop along, I see Nate let Peach inside. He turns and sees me, then jogs to meet me.

"Oh, Zelda, I'm sorry it's so cold," he says. "Come here." He picks me up, warming my frozen back paw with his hand as he carries me inside. Nate carries me to the couch; Peach has already claimed a spot on the fuzzy blanket next to Hannah. I lie next to her and let my body warm up. I lick the white stuff off my paw. Immediately it feels better.

"The cold is tough on Zelda and Peach," Nate says, taking off a layer of clothes.

"I bet," Hannah says.

"I had to carry Zelda inside because she was limping from the cold, and Peach didn't make it much farther than the door."

"Oh, geez. I guess we will do what we have to the next few days to help them out. Stupid polar vortex," Hannah says.

"You just like saying 'polar vortex'."

"So? Polar vortex is an awesome phrase." I tune them out and fall asleep.

I wake up later in the afternoon to a toy hitting me in the face. I open my eyes to see Peach flying toward me. Somehow she doesn't squash me. Instead, she rips the duck off my head and jumps back to the floor. I should join the fun, but I really need to go out first. I walk toward the back door.

"Zelda needs to go out," Ben yells.

"Okay, you need to put on her hoodie. And you need to go out with her because it's so cold. Make sure you bundle up, too," Hannah says.

"All right."

Ben grabs my hoodie, and I cooperate. I learned from my last trip that the hoodie is a good thing today. He leaves me stranded by the door as he walks upstairs.

Hurry up, people! I have to go.

After what seems like five hours, he returns downstairs with more clothes on. He opens the door.

As I walk into the yard, it feels worse than earlier.

How is that even possible?

I don't even bother running to the back fence this time. It's too cold. I find a spot on the path and run back to the door in record time. Ben lets me inside, and I run straight for Peach and the duck. I slide into the duck, grab it, and run the opposite direction. Peach chases me around the dining room table and into the living room. In the living room, I shake the duck, which slips from my mouth and goes flying into the air. Magically, it hits Peach in the head, and she stares at me dumbfounded, like I planned for that to happen.

Peach doesn't make it outside again until the darkness comes. We both run outside, ready for the coldness. This time Hannah lets us out but doesn't come with us. We both sprint our fastest to the back fence. Peach spins in about twenty circles before she does her business, then she sprints to the door. I have no idea how she can run in so many circles without falling over. A freezing blast of wind refocuses me. The hoodie barely helps in this wind. As I find the perfect spot, a sharp pain runs through my front paw.

Shoot. I wasn't fast enough.

I head for the door where Peach is waiting. She barks, telling me to hurry so we can go inside. When I don't speed up, she sprints to me and sees me walking on three legs. She barks again at me, letting me know she is going to get help. She sprints back to the door. I continue hopping along while she barks and jumps at the door. She hits the door with her head one time and then keeps on barking and jumping. Finally, someone opens it. Peach jumps and bites at what looks like Hannah's hands, then she takes off for me. When she reaches me, she sprints back to the door, which is now closed.

I feel my other paw freezing, and I know I am in trouble. I keep chugging along. This is the only time I wish we had a smaller yard. I am maybe ten pugs away.

I hear the door open again amid Peach's barks. Hannah walks outside and sends Peach in as she quickens her pace toward me. I stop and wait as she scoops me up. She carries me inside, and I let out a big sigh.

"I'm sorry, Zelda," Hannah says. "I should have gone out with you. I thought you were going to be quick like this afternoon. I'm sorry," she says again. I lick her face. I should have been quicker. It wasn't very smart of me.

Hannah sets me on the couch. Peach is playing with Lucy. I let the pain in my paws fade, and then I jump off the couch and walk to Peach. I lick her face, and then I steal the duck from her. I'm so glad Peach is looking out for me, but that's my duck!

Chapter 6
Squirrels!

The next few days remain brutally cold. Peach and I stay inside as much as possible. When we do go outside, the trips are very quick. We sleep during most of the day and darkness, dreaming about days with a warm breeze and plenty of squirrels to chase.

A few dark sleeps later, Peach and I are pleasantly surprised when we go outside without hoodies. The snow is as high as ever, but the air feels okay. It's still chilly, but we don't have to rush inside before our paws freeze. I sniff around the back fence, looking for signs of other animal life. I smell nothing except for us.

Bummer.

I head back inside.

Peach is inside waiting for me. The look in her big eyes tells me she is no longer in her sleepy phase. She is ready to play. I know I should play with her, but I am not feeling up to it. I'd rather nap for a little while longer. I am in winter hibernation mode. It's not time to wake up for spring yet! I grab a comfortable spot on the couch. I close my eyes.

Two minutes later, Peach is in my face with a skunk-tail toy. She shakes the toy, and the tail whips me in the face. I turn away from Peach and close my eyes again. I hear Peach trot up the stairs.

Good. I can have peace and quiet.

I don't make it far into my nap before the sound of owl squeaks comes bounding down the stairs. Seconds later, Peach is on the couch next to me, squeaking the owl over and over. I open my eyes and look. Her eyes are full of eager anticipation; she tells me she isn't going to give up until I play.

I drag myself up and reach for the owl. She jumps off the couch. I chase after her until my mouth grasps the owl. We play tug of war for a few minutes before I let her rip it out of my mouth. Peach takes the owl to the dog bed and lies down. I use the break in the action to reclaim my spot on the couch. Soon Peach joins me, and we sleep the morning away.

The afternoon trip outside is magical. The sun is shining, and the air feels nice on my wrinkles. I run outside to the back fence.

I smell squirrels!

For the first time in what seems like five pug years, the scent of squirrels is in the backyard. I turn to Peach, who is sniffing next to me. She looks at me, and I know we are in this together.

It's time to find the squirrels.

Peach and I take off in opposite directions, using our sniffers every step of the way. We each have to blaze our own paths through the snow. I try to eat my way through, but quickly realize my mouth isn't big enough to make a dent in the mountains of snow. My nose leads to me to a tree at the corner of the fence. The squirrel scent is flooding the tree.

Ruff. Ruff.

I look to Peach on the other side of the yard. She is barking and jumping straight into the air. I sprint to her, barking along the way. I have no idea why I am barking, but I can't resist an opportunity for the world to hear me. When I reach Peach, I look up. High in the tree is a squirrel. I can't believe Peach spotted the squirrel up there, but we have no way to reach it. I walk away disappointed.

"Zelda, Peach, inside," Nate yells. He's right; it's time to go inside. It's not quite warm enough to stay outside for hours yet.

The next afternoon we return outside for our squirrel hunt. It feels a little warmer than yesterday. I even see a few blades of grass poking through the path. We sprint straight to the back fence. The squirrel scent is overpowering. We both follow our sniffers to the tree I was investigating yesterday. A squirrel is sitting in the tree just above the fence.

Squirrel!

Peach and I go nuts—barking, jumping, anything we can do to get the squirrel to come down. The squirrel simply stares at us and squeaks.

Is that Squeaks? No, it can't be.

Squeaks was a squirrel friend of mine from our old home. He loved throwing nuts at my head. I look up, but I don't see any nuts. Peach and I both stop, unsure about what to do next. We stare at each other and then at the squirrel.

The squirrel does something unexpected. He runs down the tree onto the fence. Peach and I watch mesmerized as he runs on top of the fence. After our moment of awe, we regain our composure and start chasing him. We catch up to him in an instant because he is tiptoeing along the top of the fence to keep his balance. Peach starts leaping in the air and biting at the squirrel tail. I don't know how she does it, but she is really close to nabbing a bit of the squirrel tail.

The squirrel pauses in the corner of the fence. Then he turns and runs back the way he came.

What is he doing?

Peach chases after the squirrel again, and I follow. But I am confused. I thought he was trying to run away, but that clearly isn't the case. When the squirrel reaches the tree on the other side of the fence, he runs straight up the tree and out of Peach's leaping reach.

We catch our breath for a few minutes. Peach and I look at each other, trying to think of the next move. Once again, the squirrel beats us to the punch. He runs down the tree, back on the fence, on the same path. Peach follows again, but I stay still this time. He is up to something.

The squirrel runs along the fence to the corner. There, he turns the other way and jumps to our back neighbor's fence and climbs it. Soon he is squeaking above our heads again.

Tricky squirrels.

The squirrel isn't running away from us. He is showing us there is no way we can catch him. And every time he squeaks, he is laughing at us. I look at Peach. She is still barking. I bark to get her attention. I tell her to let him go—at least for now.

Chapter 7
The Cat Whisperer

"**D**o you want to go see Tucker and Whitney?" Ben asks.

It is the day after the squirrel incident. I tilt my head. I love going to see Tucker and Whitney. Actually, I love going to their house. I think I am invisible to Tucker and Whitney. They ignore me while I run around and play. But with Jack Jack the cat, adults and kids everywhere, a big fenced yard, and long hallways for playing, it's always an adventure at their house.

"Do you want to see Tucker and Whitney?" Ben says. I tilt my head the opposite direction.

Why is he asking me the same question twice?

I sneeze at him, run to the door, and wait for the family to get ready. Peach waits on the couch. She isn't excited because she doesn't understand. We haven't visited Tucker and Whitney since Peach came home. Eventually all six of us load up into the car and start the journey to Tucker and Whitney's house.

When we arrive, they are waiting by the front door. As usual, they greet Hannah, Nate, Ben, and Lucy, but ignore me. I think they are jealous of my curly tail. Peach tries to bring both dogs a toy, but they also ignore her.

At least I am not the only dog they ignore.

I greet Nate's dad and mom with a wagging tail and licks to the hands. Soon Peach and I are playing in the long hallway with Lucy and Ben. Tucker and Whitney jump into our game of fetch. We have a great day of fun.

When the darkness comes, I follow Lucy upstairs for bed. Midway up the stairs, Jack Jack's smell tickles my nose. I burst up the stairs and find the black fluff of cat sitting on the opposite end of the room. I run straight to him, eager to play. When I am a pug length away, I stop.

Jack Jack is hissing and turning into a puffball. I start sneezing. The puffier he gets, the more I start sneezing. I take a step toward him, risking a swat in the face. He hisses louder, and I start barking.

Why won't he play with me?

"Zelda," I hear someone yell, and footsteps approach from the stairs. Hannah is walking toward us. Jack Jack uses Hannah as a distraction and lunges for me. I leap at him, trying to grab a piece of his long, black, curly tail. My maneuver catches Jack Jack off guard; his tail smacks me in the face. I try to grab it with my mouth, but the tail is gone before I can do anything. Jack Jack darts in the direction of the gated room, but he freezes halfway to his destination. I follow his gaze to see Peach at the top of the steps. She is slowly walking toward Jack. We have him cornered.

"Zelda, leave it," Hannah says. She isn't happy with me, but I can't resist messing with, I mean, playing with Jack Jack. Peach and I remain motionless with our eyes on him. Suddenly he bolts between us and down the stairs. We give chase and crash into each other, tumbling down the steps after Jack. When we make it to the bottom, he is gone–disappeared into thin air.

Peach and I follow his scent to a small hole in a door. Peach looks at me and nudges me toward the hole. She can't fit in the hole, but I might be able to get through. I poke my head in it and see Jack Jack waiting for me at the bottom of another set of stairs. I know this is my opportunity. I have no idea what to do when I get to Jack Jack or even what I want to do. I just know I need to get to him.

I back out of the hole, get a little speed, and jump through it. It doesn't feel good as I go through, but somehow I make it. I run down the stairs toward Jack Jack. This time I don't stop when I get close. I can't control myself. Jack Jack wants no part of me. He runs the opposite direction in the basement. I chase him, but he quickly leaps onto a table in the middle of the room. I have no way up to the table; I sit on the ground looking at him.

He uses my momentary pause to leap off the table and race up the stairs. I follow, but it's too late. He is gone through the hole in the door.

Hissssss. Rufff. Rufff. Hissssss. Rufff.
Peach!

I sprint again and jump through the hole, sucking in my belly as I jump. When I cross into the room, I don't see Peach or Jack. I walk into the living room—all I see is my family, but no animals. I double back and walk upstairs, following the scent of Jack and Peach into the bedroom. Peach and Jack are lying on the bed next to each other.

What happened?

I jump onto the bed. Nobody moves. Peach nods. I walk over to Jack Jack. I start sneezing again, but he doesn't budge. I am unsure what to do next. Since I am a pug, I figure a nap is as good of an idea as any other. I lie down next to Peach and Jack Jack. Jack Jack moves his head so it's resting on my body. I smile as my eyes grow heavy.

The rest of the trip is a barrel of fun between Peach, Jack Jack, and me. We play hide-and-seek throughout the house. I enjoy every minute, but wonder through it all what happened between Peach and Jack Jack. I don't think I will ever know.

Chapter 8
The Chase

When we return home from Tucker and Whitney's house, I see more grass peeking through the snow. Two or three dark sleeps after our trip, we walk outside to a beautiful day. The sun is shining, keeping it warm so my paws won't get cold, but it's not too hot either. It's perfect pug-walking weather, and I am ready to explore the neighborhood.

The family is gone for the day, except for Hannah. I wait by the front door most of the day, hoping she will take me for a walk. She ignores me, or maybe she doesn't get the hint. Either way, I wait and hope my big pug eyes will give her the right idea.

Eventually I fall asleep, and I wake up to the door being opened. I jump up and out of the way as the door flies toward me. Ben and Lucy skip into the house. Peach jumps off the couch to greet them.

"Hi, Mom," Lucy says.

"How was your day?" Hannah asks.

"Boring," Ben says as he receives four licks to the face from Peach.

"It was good," Lucy says. Lucy takes off her coat and bends over to take off her shoes.

I don't want her to take off her shoes!

I run over and grab hold of her shoestrings.

"Hi, Zelda," Lucy says, petting my head. I let the strings fall and lick her face.

"Do you want to go for a walk, Zelda?" Lucy asks. I jump, sneeze, and lick her face simultaneously. I don't think I could do that ever again.

"Okay. Let's ask Mom," she says. "Hey, Mom, can we take the dogs for a walk? Zelda told me she wants to go."

"Zelda told you that?" Ben asks. "I didn't know dogs could talk."

"Zelda talks to me," Lucy says.

"Hey, Ben, be nice to your sister," Hannah replies. "And yes, why don't all of us take the dogs for a walk?"

"Yay!" Lucy shouts.

Ben grabs the harnesses and snatches me as I try to circle him. When everyone is harnessed and ready to go, Ben hands my leash to Hannah. He opens the door, and my excitement propels me forward at lightning speed. In an instant, I jerk backward.

Stupid leash.

I lead the way with Hannah, Ben, Peach, and Lucy behind me. The sidewalks are clear except for some water. The white stuff still covers most of the grass, but it's only halfway up my paws. I head for the first great spot, the big tree a few houses down.

"Zelda, slow down," I hear Hannah yell.

I can't slow down! There are so many places to investigate!

I stop at the big tree. Peach joins me, and we sniff together. I smell dog and squirrel mostly.

"Mom, can I walk Peach?" Lucy asks.

"I don't know, Peach is pretty strong," Hannah says.

"Lucy will be fine. Peach doesn't pull like Zelda," Ben says.

"Please," Lucy says.

"Okay. Here you go. Just hang on tight," Hannah says.

I move on down the street, stopping when my nose tells me. We reach the corner quickly. Peach leads the way forward with Lucy. I trail behind for a minute to check out the light post.

Rufff Rufff!

"Peach, no!" Lucy shouts.

I look up and see Peach at a full sprint. She is chasing a squirrel through a yard, her leash flailing on the ground behind her. I bark; she looks like she is having so much fun.

"Peach," Ben and Hannah yell simultaneously.

"Go get Peach, Ben. I have Zelda," Hannah says. Ben sprints forward, trying to catch Peach. Peach has left the yard and rounded the corner back toward home. I can't see the squirrel anywhere; I have no idea where it went.

"I'm sorry, Mom. I lost Peach," Lucy says. Her eyes begin to well up with water.

"It's okay, Lucy, let's go help your brother," Hannah says. "C'mon, Zelda, let's go." We jog in the direction of Ben. I hear Ben yelling for Peach, but I can't see her anywhere. I know Peach wouldn't run away, but she doesn't know the neighborhood yet.

What if she gets lost?

Ben is only a few houses down from us. We are gaining ground on him. He is still yelling for Peach. I see her. She is out of his reach, but not much farther ahead.

"Mom, why don't you try to get her. Peach isn't listening to me. I can take Zelda," he says.

"Okay." Hannah hands Ben my leash and takes some quick steps forward. I hear Lucy sniffling behind us.

"Don't worry about it, Lucy. Peach is fine, we will catch up to her," Ben says. She doesn't say anything.

"Peach, come here," Hannah says. When Peach is within Hannah's grasp, Peach runs a little bit farther. I watch this scene repeated over and over. I start to smile. Peach isn't going anywhere. She just doesn't want to be on the leash again.

We keep walking forward, and before we know it, we are only a few houses down from ours. I keep walking, urging Ben forward. Maybe if we get ahead, Peach will know to go home.

"Good girl," Hannah says. Peach is standing on the steps of our front door, waiting to be let inside. Hannah walks behind her and lets Peach in. We walk through the doors. Lucy runs straight for Peach and hugs her.

"I'm sorry I let you go," Lucy says.

"Sorry, Mom, I didn't think Peach would go after a squirrel like Zelda does," Ben says, taking off my harness.

Why wouldn't Peach chase after a squirrel? She's a dog!

"It's okay, Ben," Hannah says. "It all worked out this time. And now we know Lucy can't walk Peach."

Chapter 9
The Race Track

After the brief respite from the cold and snow, both return with a vengeance. Peach and I return to our playdays inside. We stay out of the frigid tundra of a backyard and look for adventures inside the house. It's not too exciting until Ben begins assembling something in the living room.

Peach and I watch from the couch as he dumps the contents of a box on the living room floor. A bunch of parts and pieces scatter. I get up to investigate. They come in a few different shapes and sizes. When Ben turns his back, I grab one of the pieces and run into the corner and away from his gaze. I smell the piece first, but I don't smell anything I recognize. I slowly put it in my mouth. It doesn't have a good taste, but it feels a little like a Nylabone on my teeth. Although it's much harder to chew. I spit it out and walk back to Ben.

I watch Ben take the pieces and smash them together. Somehow they stick to make a bigger piece. He repeats this process over and over. I am entranced by it; I can't look away.

"Peach, what do you have?" Ben asks. I see Peach in the corner, and I hear her teeth grinding. Peach ignores Ben and keeps chewing.

I don't think Peach should be chewing on that.

"Peach," Ben says again. He walks to Peach and grabs the piece from her mouth. Peach's big eyes follow him back to his spot on the floor. He continues smashing the pieces together. After a few more minutes watching Ben, my eyes start to droop. I lay my head on the floor.

Vrrooooom.

I am jerked awake from my slumber. I turn my head to the noise. It's coming from Ben, no wait, from the smashed pieces. But now the pieces are one giant, dark strip curving over the floor. Peach is staring at the strip like it's a squirrel.

Wait a second, something is moving.

Peach leaps toward the black strip.

Is it a tiny squirrel?

I get closer, trying to figure out what is moving. Peach keeps leaping, and Ben is laughing at her.

I see it.

It looks like a miniature car. Whatever it is, I want to get it before Peach does. I set up camp opposite her and try to catch the car with my paw.

It's faster than I thought!

I better use my mouth. I chase the car around and try to nab it with my mouth. I feel the coldness and hardness of the car on my teeth for an instant before I lose it.

The car turns so quickly!

I wait and watch the car this time. I let it circle toward Peach before I go for it. Peach has a different idea, and we collide heads when we both reach for it. Both our heads are hard as rocks, but I have lots of wrinkles to cushion me from head-butts. Peach, on the other hand, looks dazed. I look for the car.

Vrrooooom.

"Here you go, Zelda and Peach, get it!" Ben says. I wait and watch the car. It takes all my pug patience to not run for it, but I know watching will give me clues how to catch it. The car is curving through the track on a pattern. It goes by Ben and then circles back to Peach before running by me. The only straight section is in front of Ben. I move over to him and wait. I see it coming from around the corner. I pounce on it like a cat. My paws cover the strip. The car runs into my paw, and I grab the car with my mouth.

I got it!

I run with it through the house. Peach chases me, eager to get her paws on it.

"Zelda, wait," Ben yells. It's too late. We are gone. I run up the stairs, and Peach chases me. I run through the bedrooms upstairs and back down the stairs. I jump on the couch and sit, out of breath.

"Zelda, drop it," Ben says. I drop the car, and he takes it from me. Ben brings the car back to the dark strip.

Vrrooooom.

The car starts running, and Peach jumps on the ground after it. I let her go for it. I know the pattern now anyway. After a minute or so, she grabs the car and releases it. She looks at me on the couch, and I look at her. I know exactly what she is thinking. That was fun while it lasted, but nowhere near as fun as squirrel chases.

Chapter 10
Squirrels – Part 2

P each and I hear the birds chirping today, signaling the start of warm afternoons filled with green grass and sunshine. The birds always know before pugs when it shifts to warm days. Even though we haven't seen any squirrels in our yard for a long time, we start searching for signs. I detect a faint whiff of squirrel lingering in the backyard, but no sign of any recent visits.

Without squirrels to hunt, Peach and I chase each other through the yard. We create our own trails in the snow, and over the course of a few days, the grass is visible again. I see birds hanging out in the trees high above us; the squirrels will be returning soon.

Inside the house, Hannah brings home a new toy for us—a squeaky squirrel. The squirrel looks real, and the squeak is louder than the owl's! We play with the squirrel for hours each day. Peach even tries to bring it outside with us, but Hannah doesn't let her.

A few days after the fake squirrel comes home, the scent is back. Our squirrel nemesis has returned. I find the scent in one corner, and Peach traces it along the fence to the other side of the yard. The smell is fresh; we probably just missed him. The squirrel scent excites us. Peach runs full speed at me with crazy eyes. I duck out of her way in the nick of time, and she sails past me. I turn and chase her through the yard. We run full speed to all corners of the yard three times before we take a break. We eat several mouthfuls of snow and cool off.

Squeak. Squeak. Squeak.

Our heads turn in unison to the source of the squeak. A squirrel is sitting in a tree in our neighbor's yard, looking down on us.

He is back!

Peach and I look at each other and then dash to the fence. The squirrel squeaks at us for a few minutes. We bark back, baiting the squirrel to come down. He moves down the tree, and in one solid leap he is on the fence running to the other side. We give chase to the squirrel, putting our plan in action.

Peach runs to the other side of the yard. I keep running with the squirrel. He runs up the tree in our yard and stops high above me.

Squeak. Squeak. Squeak.

The squirrel is taunting me, and I play his game. I bark at him, jumping as high as I can, knowing there is no way I will reach him. The squirrel leaps from one branch to another, lower and lower. I have to admit that it's an impressive feat. He jumps on the fence and runs to where he started.

I follow him for a few pug lengths and stop so I don't get in the way. Peach is barreling along the fence line toward me. When she is a few pug lengths away, she leaps into the air. I have never seen Peach jump this high; her head is above the fence! The squirrel is coming straight at her. Everything is moving in slow motion. At the last instant, the squirrel tries to turn, but it is too late. Peach grabs hold of his tail, and she sails to the ground with the squirrel.

Peach and the squirrel crash in the snowy grass. The impact causes Peach to lose her grip on the squirrel. But the squirrel is stunned. He doesn't move. I approach slowly as Peach rolls over, shakes off, and stands up. I can tell she is stunned.

I am less than a pug length away when the squirrel awakens from his daze. He looks at Peach and me and then bolts to the front yard. I chase after him, but he runs under the fence on the side of the yard.

I can't believe what just happened. I thought our plan was perfect. Peach was magnificent, flying through the air and grabbing the squirrel. But we forgot the landing would be tough.

We were so close! Those pesky squirrels.

Chapter 11
The House Guest

"When is Norman coming over?" Ben asks.
Norman?

"Soon." Hannah says.

Norman is a family friend. He was my best friend until Peach came home. Norman is much bigger than Peach or me—I think seven pugs put together equal one Norman. His head is almost the size of me, and it is just as wrinkly as a pug head. We have lots of fun playing together, even if he is seven times my size. Norman comes to visit us with his family, and sometimes we go to his house. But I haven't seen Norman in a while—Peach hasn't met him yet!

I don't know what to do with myself while I wait. I walk around bringing toys to everyone in the house, but everyone is busy. I find a bone and start chewing. Chewing always makes the time go by fast.

A door slams outside; I jump on the couch to look out the window.

Norman is here!

I run to the front door and wait. Peach senses my excitement. She barks a few times before joining me at the door. She starts barking as Norman's scent approaches. We can't see a thing through the door. Finally, Hannah opens the door, and Norman runs inside. He slides into the wall, but he keeps running. He checks out every room in the house, upstairs and down, before he greets me in the living room.

Peach approaches Norman cautiously. Norman lets her sniff him, and after a quick meet and greet, it's off to the races. Peach grabs a toy, and Norman chases after her. I wait for them to return to the room before I jump into the fun.

I realize a few hours later that Norman's family left him at our house. They didn't stay like usual. When the darkness comes, I expect for his family to take him home, but they never arrive. Instead, Norman, Peach, and I head upstairs for bed.

"Where is Norman sleeping?" Ben asks.

"We haven't worked that out, but we are guessing on the floor in our bedroom," Nate says.

"Can he sleep in my room?" Ben replies.

"Sure, but you need to keep your door closed. We don't want him roaming around the house at night," Nate says.

"Okay!"

I am happy Norman is spending more time with us and even happier that he won't be sleeping in an already crowded bed with Peach, Lucy, and me.

When I wake up, only a faint stream of light is peeking through the window. Peach and I walk to the back door to go outside. Norman must be sleeping still. The sky is gray, the air is cool, and water is falling from the sky. Peach and I hurry so we can get into the dry, warm house.

Norman bounds into the living room a few minutes later. He grabs the nearest toy and starts a round of chase with Peach. I watch from the couch; I could use a few more hours of sleep.

The day is filled with many more games of chase in the house. Peach and I team up in tug of war against Norman, but he wins every time with his huge mouth. By the time the darkness comes, Peach and I are exhausted. Norman, on the other hand, could play for another five hours straight. He is an energetic dog. I don't know how he does it all day.

After a full day with Norman, I also notice the consequences of his huge mouth. He drools and slobbers on everything. All of our toys now are slimy and slippery. He also loves chewing and destroying our toys. I don't think he means to do it, but our toys are designed for pug-sized mouths, not Norman's gigantic face. It makes me realize how glad I am to have Peach as a sister since we are similar kinds of dogs. Even if she doesn't have the curly tail or as many wrinkles, her face is still half-smashed, and she's the same size as a pug.

The next day I wake up to bright light. I run downstairs, and Hannah lets me out into a bright, sunshine-filled day. It's a little cold outside, but warm enough for all three of us to play outside.

We spend the morning inside, mostly napping and chewing. We wore Norman out more than I thought. Maybe he isn't used to chasing one dog around, let alone two!

After a morning of naps, I wait by the door. Peach follows my lead.

"Can I let the dogs out?" Ben asks.

"Just Zelda and Peach," Hannah says.

"Why not Norman?" Ben responds.

"All three of them will play in the backyard together."

"So? I don't understand the problem, Mom."

"I don't want them to come inside a muddy mess. It rained all day yesterday."

"Oh. Let me go check the yard. It may have dried enough with the sun. If it's dry, can I let Norman out with us?"

"Okay. Just make sure there's no mud," Hannah says.

A few minutes later, Ben lets us outside. I wander to the back fence and accidentally sink into a puddle. I turn around to investigate a drier area. Ben walks out the door, says a few words to Hannah, and then yells for Norman. Norman comes running outside and straight for me at a full sprint. I run the other direction, and the game begins. Peach joins us in the second lap. I am the slowest of the three but the only dog who can maneuver sharp turns without tumbling. Norman is super fast with his long legs, but he doesn't have good control of his body. Peach is almost as quick as Norman, but she can't corner as well as I can.

Somehow I end up in the lead of the chase. I lead them toward the back, then turn sharply before the squishy puddle area. I run the other direction. I hear Peach following behind me and turn my head in time to see Norman. He tries to make the quick turn but loses his footing. His paws slide out from underneath him, and he lands on his back. He slides for a few seconds before he regains his footing, gets up, and runs toward us. He is covered in dirt and mud and water. I stop and stare. Ben starts laughing. Norman slows down and approaches us, panting with his tongue hanging out.

"Ben!" Hannah is standing outside now. "I thought the yard wasn't muddy!" she yells.

"I'm sorry, Mom. I didn't think that would happen. Can you get me a towel? Maybe two or three?" Ben says. After Ben cleans Norman, we spend the rest of the day inside. Norman is pretty tired; I think he got a little banged up from his tumble. When the dark comes, Norman's family arrives. Peach and I say good-bye to him. Even with the mud and slobber, it was a fantastic weekend.

Chapter 12
The Easter Egg Hunt

"**C**'mon, Ben and Lucy," Hannah says. "It's time to go, we don't want to be late."

"Can Peach and Zelda come to the Easter Egg Hunt with us?" Lucy asks.

"Nate, do you think it's okay to bring the dogs?"

"It's outside at a park. I'm sure it will be fine," Nate says. I look at Peach. Her ears are standing straight up. She wants to go to the park, too. We both jump off the couch and sprint for the door.

"Dad, I think Z and Peach want to come!" Ben says, laughing.

"I'll go grab some treats and water for the dogs. Then I'm ready to go," Hannah says.

When we step outside at the park, I feel a warm breeze rustle through my fur. I know pugs aren't warm-weather dogs, but after the long winter, the warm air feels great.

The park is crawling with people. I am so overwhelmed by all the scents that I don't know where to start.

"Hannah, why don't you take the kids to the Egg Hunt area. I'll find a good spot to watch with the dogs where they won't cause too much trouble," Nate says. I smell something tasty to my left. I try to pull Nate left as Peach heads the other direction.

"Okay, dear. Let's go get some Easter eggs!" Hannah says. Hannah, Ben, and Lucy walk in the direction of all the people.

"Okay, pups, why don't we find a place to sit on the hill over there?" Nate says. Nate steers us away from the crowd of people. I don't mind; I have plenty of smells to investigate before I will even think about meeting new people. We end up on a hill and looking down on the crowd. We aren't too far away; I look for my family, and I find them on the edge of the crowd. I see a smile on Lucy's face, and I know they are fine. In front of the crowd is a wide-open field of grass. Small balls or maybe toys are scattered everywhere on the field.

Strange.

I turn my attention back to my area. Peach and I use as much leash as we can to explore. I smell dogs, squirrels, and even a cat or two when I hear a high-pitched whistle.

I look down below. The crowd is dispersing into the field of balls in a hurry. I spot Lucy and Ben moving together; they are picking up as many as they can. Hannah is still on the edge of the field.

I want to help!

I look at Nate. He has relaxed his grip on the leashes.

Should I go for it?

I am ready to bolt when Peach sits down next to me. I look at her and then shift my gaze to Lucy. Peach barks. I bark back. We go for it.

I use all of my pug strength to put force into my run. I expect to be yanked backward at any moment, but it doesn't happen. I keep running. Peach is right beside me, and we are flying down the hill toward Lucy. I don't see Ben; they must have separated. We reach them within minutes.

"Hi, Peach. Hi, Zelda. Want to help collect Easter eggs?" she says.

Yes!

I grab the closest ball I see. It's a little big for my tiny pug mouth, but I get the right grip and bring it back to Lucy. I drop it in front of her.

"Thanks, Z Bug," she says, unhooking my leash.

Freedom!

I'm running for the next ball when I remember Peach. I turn and look back at Lucy. Peach is by her side, chewing on the ball. Or egg, or whatever it is.

I guess I am on my own. I better get moving.

I race around the field grabbing as many eggs for Lucy as I can. I avoid the outstretched arms of other kids and adults. I hear my name being called, but I ignore it. Peach gives up chewing on her egg and runs with me the next several times. Her leash trails behind her. After a few minutes, we have brought Lucy eight eggs, but I see Nate approaching Lucy.

Oh, no.

"Zelda, Peach, come," he yells. I don't want to go to him. I'm having so much fun. Peach looks at me and then walks to Nate. Nate grabs her leash.

"Good girl, Peach."

Now I am really in trouble.

I run in the opposite direction for one more egg. I hear Nate yell my name again, but I don't care. I snatch an egg and run back to Lucy in a matter of minutes.

"Thanks, Zelda," she says. She bends over and pets me. I lick her face. Nate walks over and leashes me. He doesn't say a word.

"How did Z and Peach get away?" Ben says as he approaches with his mom.

"I don't know," Nate says. Ben laughs.

"So you weren't paying attention," Hannah says.

"Maybe. But I didn't take Z's leash off her." Everyone turns to Lucy.

"She was helping me!" Lucy says.

"It's okay. They didn't do any harm to anyone," Nate says.

"You weren't on the sidelines with all the parents," Hannah says. "You would have thought two bears were running through the field with the comments I heard."

"Mom, I won a special prize!" Lucy says. "Look!" She handed her mom an egg.

"Yes you did! You need to go see the Easter Bunny to get it. C'mon let's head that way," Hannah says.

"Hold on tight," Nate says to Ben, handing him my leash.

We wander over to another section of the park and wait. After a few minutes, a stranger arrives.

"Congrats," the stranger says. "Oh, and look at your cute dogs. I heard a dog was running through the Easter Egg Hunt. It definitely couldn't have been these two cuties." She bends down and pets us. "Okay, you get to pick out something from the big chocolate bunny box." Lucy searches through the box and pulls something out.

"And now you can go meet the Easter Bunny. You should be next, right around the table," the stranger says. We walk around the corner, and I freeze in my pug tracks.

I am staring at a giant rabbit. The rabbit is bigger than Nate or Hannah. It is standing on two feet, not four. It's the strangest sight I have ever seen. Lucy starts walking toward it.

Noooooooo!

I bark furiously at Lucy to get her attention. I lunge toward her, but Ben is holding on tight. Peach isn't making a sound. In fact, she is busy sniffing the ground. While I am barking, Nate scoops me off the ground into his arms. I squirm, but he is too strong.

"I think Zelda has fear of the Easter Bunny," Nate says. I resign to watching the terror take place. Lucy stands next to the rabbit. The rabbit puts his leg or maybe his arm around Lucy. I am terrified about what is going to happen next.

"Smile, Lucy," Hannah says. And then it's over. Lucy walks away from the mutant rabbit unharmed. We walk away from the rabbit, away from the people, and back to our car. I never want to see that rabbit again! I think it could eat me.

"Did you have fun, Lucy?" Hannah asks.

"Yes, I loved it!"

"And Ben?"

"Are you kidding me? It was hilarious watching Zelda and Peach!" Ben says.

"Yeah, it was pretty funny," Hannah says. "Hopefully they still invite us to the next neighborhood party."

"And if not, oh well," Nate says. "At least we have a great story to tell."

"We sure do. It's always an adventure with Zelda," Hannah says.

"And Peach!" Lucy says.

Chapter 13
Zelda's Fourth Birthday

Today is a big day for me—it's my fourth birthday. My fourth birthday marks two years since Hannah and Nate brought me home to their family. I can't believe it's only been two years. I feel like I've been here forever. I barely remember my life before Hannah, Nate, Ben, and Lucy. Honestly, I am not sure I want to remember those days anyway.

It's a little strange because I haven't heard my family mention my birthday much. Usually I catch snippets of conversation and listen to the plans for me. But not a peep. I hope they didn't forget about my birthday! Last year I had a feast on my birthday-new toys, bacon with dinner, and a new bone.

My birthday starts like any other day. Peach and I wake up and slowly make our way downstairs. We go through our morning ritual of going outside, eating breakfast, and a round or two of the mouth game. When we grow tired, we snuggle with each other on the couch. We lounge around the house for the day while Ben, Lucy, and Nate are away.

When Lucy and Ben arrive home with Hannah, Lucy runs straight to me.

"Happy Birthday Zelda pug!" she says, giving me a big squeeze. "Sorry I forgot this morning," she whispers. I lick her face, happy someone remembered my birthday.

"Mom, can we take the dogs for a walk?" Lucy asks.

"Sure," she replies. "Ben, can you come, too?"

"Yeah, I can do that," he says. "Can we go now though? I wanted to go over to Jack's house before the party later."

"Okay. C'mon, Lucy, let's get the dogs harnessed," Hannah says.

Since it's my birthday, I decide to show the family my pug best. I walk right to Hannah and allow her to put the harness on me without a fight or running in circles.

We take our normal route around the neighborhood. Surprisingly, the street is pretty quiet. We don't see any squirrels, only a few people, and no other dogs. I try to prolong the walk by resting under a tree. But after a minute, my family is dragging me forward again. Peach walks beside me trying to catch birds. I never go after birds; it seems silly since they can fly. Peach thinks she is quick enough to leap and catch one, but she hasn't come close yet. Being on a leash definitely hurts her chances, too.

When we return home, I stick my head into the water bowl. I gave up long ago trying to drink water without getting my head wet. It's impossible because of my flat face and small tongue. I just take the plunge.

"Happy Birthday, Zelda!" Nate says, walking into the house. He gives me a few pets before greeting the rest of the family.

"Oh, good, you are home just in time for dinner," Hannah says.

"Dinner already?"

"Yes, we are eating early so we can make the meet up," she says.

"Oh, yeah, of course. How could I forget?"

The family files into the living room. Peach and I follow them and resume our normal spots during dinner. Peach sits under the table while I sit in front of Nate's chair, waiting for table food.

"Oh, wait, don't we have some special treats around?" Nate says.

Treats! I love treats!

"Yeah, check the cabinet of dog stuff over there." I follow Nate, jumping on his heels as he checks out the treat closet. He fills my bowl with deliciousness, and I chow down. The treats are moist and meaty, and I can't get enough. I finish the bowl quickly and look up. I see Peach eating her portion next to me.

Hey, it's my birthday, not Peach's!

I try to squeeze my way into Peach's bowl, but I realize it's too late. She has finished her bowl, too. I lick the remaining crumbs dry before returning to my spot by Nate's feet in the dining room. Nate slips me a piece of chicken under the table. I knew he would give me table food on my birthday.

"Hannah, anything we need to bring tonight?" Nate asks as they clean up the table after dinner.

"Just the dogs. Maybe some water and treats, just in case."

"All right, well let's get moving," he says.

Ben walks over to the harnesses.

"All right, Zelda, are you ready to go for a ride?" Ben asks.

Ride? Where are we going? Dog store? Norman's house? Park?

I run around the coffee table four times before I calm down enough to let Ben harness and leash me. Peach, of course, walks right over and is leashed. We load up the car, and I sit in Lucy's lap.

"Zelda, are you excited?" she whispers while she pets me. "You get to meet more pugs."

Wait a minute, did she say pugs?

I leap to the other side, barging over Peach, and I look out the other window. No sign of pugs anywhere. I sit down and look at Peach. Her calm eyes tell me to wait, to be patient.

A few minutes later, we get out of the car. The first thing I notice is the smell of dogs. It's overwhelming. Then I hear the barking. I look to the source, but I can't see through the maze of cars. I pull my family toward the smell and noise. As we approach, my nose tells me the smell is mostly pug. We burst through the pack of cars, and in front of me is a large, fenced area. Inside are a number of dogs, most of which are wrinkly, flat-faced, and curly tailed pugs! I run for the fence.

"Wait, Zelda," someone yells. I stop. Peach walks beside me. She is smiling. I know she is excited, too, although I'm guessing she wished all the dogs didn't look like me. Nate leads me into the fence of pugs.

"Happy Birthday, Zelda!" he says and lets me off the leash. I run for the first pug I see, then move on to the next and the next. I count at least ten pugs as I greet everyone with sniffs and barks. I start a pug chase, and all of us are running after each other with our tails bouncing and wrinkles jiggling. After a few minutes, I lie down panting with my tongue hanging out of my mouth. I look around for Peach. I see a dark pug chasing her around the fence. She is barely running—she is so much faster than all of us, even me. I bark for her. She turns and finds me, then walks over. I get up and bite at her leg. She bites back, and soon we are tumbling through the grass. Somehow, a pair of pugs ends up next to us and joins the fun.

This is the best birthday gift ever. I haven't seen any pugs since I moved in with Hannah and Nate. I thought I might be the last remaining pug. I am glad I am not. It is great to be in the company of all these sneezing, snorting dogs—it makes me feel normal again.

Chapter 14
A Long Trip

When the bags start appearing in each room of the house, I know something is about to happen. I hear the family mention "vacation" a few times as they fill their bags. My family disappeared for a week or so on a "vacation" some time ago; I was left behind with Hannah's mom. At least if that happens again, I will have Peach by my side.

Even with the appearance of the bags, the day continues like any other. Peach and I get a morning and afternoon walk. We play in the house with Ben. We eat dinner. We beg for more food. When the darkness comes, we collapse on Lucy's bed. Hannah and Nate come in to say good night to us.

"Good night. Sleep well. We leave early tomorrow morning," Hannah says. She gives Lucy a kiss and pets us before leaving the room. Nate does the same. As I fall asleep, I wonder where my family is going tomorrow and if I am going with them.

"Wake up! Rise and shine!" Nate says to us. I don't even open my eyes. It's way too early for a pug to be awake. I hear a groan of agreement from Peach at the foot of the bed.

"C'mon, Lucy. We need to get on the road. You can sleep in the car." Lucy stirs and slowly rises.

"You, too, Zelda and Peach. Time to go outside," Nate says. *Outside* gets our attention. Peach and I jump off the bed and follow Nate downstairs. When we come back inside, the family is waiting for us.

"Ready to go?" Hannah says with a cup in her hand.

"I'm as ready as I can be at five-thirty a.m.," Nate says.

"All right, let's load up." We load up into the car. As soon as we start moving, my eyes feel heavy. Lucy has a blanket. I snuggle with her and fall asleep.

I wake up to the car stopping. I look out the window, but I don't recognize a thing. Ben leashes us, and we jump onto the warm ground. It's bright outside, but I can't tell how long I have been sleeping. Ben hands us off to Nate and walks inside the building. Nate takes us to some grass and gives us water.

"All right, time to get back in the car. We still have a ways to go." We walk back into the car. Hannah, Lucy, and Ben are already there. Peach takes my blanket spot, so I jump in the front and find a spot on Hannah's lap. The hypnotic rhythm of the car puts me back to sleep in no time.

Once again I wake up to the car stopping. Almost the same scene happens as at the last stop. I feel like I am dreaming, but I notice different smells, so I know we must be somewhere new. Peach looks confused, too, but I have no idea what to tell her. When we get back in the car, Peach is shaking. I curl up next to her to let her know everything will be okay.

When we start moving, I try to fall asleep, but my pug brain is on overdrive. I find myself pacing from one lap to the next, trying to see what's happening outside. Mostly I see cars and some trees.

"Zelda, come here," Ben says. I walk to him, and he sets me in his lap, trapping me. I look at Peach, and then I hear her snore.

At least she is sleeping.

I sit down for a few minutes before I grow restless. Ben lets me stand and look out the window. As I watch all the cars, I begin to grow dizzy. I sit again for a while, but I keep checking outside to see if I notice anything familiar. At one point, all I can see out the window is blue. But besides that, it's all new.

After what seems like forever, we start to slow down. We end up in a neighborhood with lots of houses. When we pull into a house, I start jumping around the car. It's finally time to get out.

Peach and I sprint out the door. We are immediately blasted by the heat. I start goose-honking to catch my breath in the hot, humid air. We follow our family inside the house. Peach and I run through the house, investigating every nook and cranny. I don't smell any traces of dogs or cats. The house is a little smaller than our house, but I like it because most of the floor isn't slippery.

After my initial house investigation, I find my family in the big room by the door. Peach is chewing on a bone.

Where did she get that?

I look in the room and see the basket of toys from home has appeared by the wall. I walk over and grab a bone of my own while the rest of the family is talking. As I start chewing, I look at the bags piled by the door, and a question pops up in my wrinkles.

What if we aren't going home?

I don't know how I feel about staying since we just got here. But with Peach and my family here, I'm sure it will be okay.

Chapter 15
The Beach

Peach and I wake up the next day ready for a full day of adventures. We didn't have time yesterday to explore outside. Nate and Ben take us for a walk first thing in the morning. It isn't quite as warm as yesterday, at least not yet, and the wind is blowing. The wind feels nice as we walk. The ground is very soft; my paws sink into the dirt. I like the soft dirt; it is fun to walk in it. I notice a few trees, but the trees look different from the squirrel trees at the old house. The smells are different, too. I catch faint whiffs of dogs and cats, but no squirrel or anything else I recognize.

Rufff.

I look toward Peach, who is several pugs ahead of me. She is staring straight ahead. I look in the direction and see something unfamiliar. It looks like water, but it's moving, and we are heading right toward it.

As we approach the water, the soft, dry dirt turns into goopy, wet dirt. The water is moving. It moves toward us and then fades away before returning. I've never seen water move like this or seen so much water at once. All I see is water as I look forward. It doesn't end.

Besides drinking, I'm not the biggest fan of water because my fur is like a sponge. Once I'm wet, it takes forever for me to dry. Peach, on the other hand, dries right away.

Peach is wandering toward the water. She takes a few steps in it, but it comes rushing forward, and she runs backward. She plays that game for a few minutes before she leads me into the water. We splash around. She is right; the water feels great. We are having so much fun that we don't see the huge rush of water coming at us. I turn and see it when it's mere seconds away. I bark quickly to warn Peach before I start running.

I'm too late.

The water rushes over my small body. Somehow, I manage to keep my head above the water as it runs past. And then as fast as it came, it's gone. I look to Peach. She's panting and smiling, but barely wet.

"Did you see that?" Ben says.

"Yes! That was incredible." Nate says.

"Peach just jumped over the wave—completely missed it." Ben says.

Why didn't I think of that? Now I am soaked and weigh five more pounds in water weight.

"Poor Zelda," Nate says. "She's a mess."

I wander back to very edge of the water and sit. I watch the water rush back and forth. Peach continues to chase the water and leap through it. It is fun here on the water's edge. Even though I'm wet, I'm not cold because it's so warm outside. I drift off to pug dreamland.

"Zelda, time to go," Ben says. I get up and walk with the gang back to the house. When we get there, I am immediately taken to the bathroom. Hannah washes all the dirt off me, and I shake clean in the tub. She hates when I do that, but it feels so good. I find Lucy on the couch. Hannah brings me a dry towel. I fall asleep.

The next few days are great. Peach and I play in the water in the morning, and then we relax in the afternoon at home. Often the family goes away during the afternoon, so we have free reign of the house. We run all over the place, jumping on every bed and chair in the house. In the evening, we spend time with the family. We often go for dark-time walks on the street and sidewalks.

I begin adjusting to the new home and routine. It's very different than home, much more relaxed. The family has more time with us, but it's so hot during the day that I can't be outside for very long. Although the water does help.

After another relaxing day, the whole family is sitting in the living room.

"Why don't we get out of here and go for a evening walk at the beach?" Nate says.

"That sounds good. We can bring some kites to fly. Sound okay?" Hannah turns to Ben and Lucy.

"Yeah, I want to fly a kite!" Lucy says.

"Can we bring the dogs?" Ben asks.

"Sure," Nate says.

We head to the beach. Lucy and Hannah stay on the dirt while Ben, Nate, Peach, and I head for the water's edge. Peach and I chase the water. The water is coming faster and bigger than normal. I pay close attention. When

I see a big wave coming, I bark. Peach looks at me, and then we both jump.

I did it! I jumped over it!

Splash!

Another rush of water crashes into me, soaking my belly.

Whoops. I forgot the water keeps coming.

Peach and I play in the water for a few more minutes, but it's getting darker outside. Ben and Nate notice the approaching darkness; they lead us toward Hannah and Lucy.

As we walk on the dry, soft dirt, I notice a trace of movement in front of me. I walk toward it, and something scurries away.

What is that?

I bark for Peach, and she walks to me. We venture forth together, looking for signs of movement. I see a flash out of the corner of my eye. Peach runs for it but misses it. She has no clue what it is, either.

I see a small creature scurrying, and I run for it. I miss catching it with my mouth, but I get a glimpse of it this time. I have never seen anything like it. The animal has lots of legs and is a light color that matches the dirt. It looks like a bug, but it's much bigger than any bug I've seen.

Arrrfff!

That's not a good sign. I turn and run to Peach. She's only a few steps away and is licking her paw. I turn and look for movement again. I need to figure out what these creatures are. I see movement and bolt. I'm catching this thing. I lunge my mouth for it and get it. The creature pinches me.

Owwww. Yikes!

Instinctively, I let it go. Peach and I run for the street, away from the soft dirt and pinching creatures.

"I guess they didn't want to chase the crabs anymore," Nate says. "It's time to go anyway. It's getting dark, and soon the crabs will be everywhere on this beach." Hannah and Lucy join us, and we walk to our new home.

For the next two days, Peach and I stay away from the water when it gets dark. During the morning, we enjoy every second on the water's edge. When I see the bags appear again, I realize that we are going home. This was only a trip, an adventure with the whole family somewhere new.

We spend the next day in the car. I have lots of time to dream about bacon and squirrels. I also think about my pug life. I can be happy anywhere as long as I am with my family, especially Peach. When I met Peach for the first time on Christmas morning, I was ecstatic to have a sister, even if the first few weeks were an adjustment. Over time, Peach and I have learned how to get along, to share toys, to go on walks, and to adventure together. Most important, we have learned to trust each other. Peach and I are best friends. More than that, we are sisters, even if she doesn't have a curly tail!

Chapter 16
Epilogue: A Peach Tale

My life was a blur before moving in with Zelda. I spent many days in a cage without toys or the chance to stretch my legs. Three or four times I had puppies, but after a few weeks all of my puppies were taken away from me. I was always really sad to lose my puppies. Luckily, one day I was released from the cage to a few nice people. They took me home and took care of me for a few weeks.

When I met Nate for the first time, I was terrified because I had adapted to my new home. I had a few dog brothers and sisters to play with in the backyard. I didn't want to be taken back to my life in the cage. But after a few minutes with Nate, I knew it would be okay. He was so nice; he had a big smile on his face as he rubbed my belly.

I entered my new (and hopefully final) home with Nate that night. I immediately knew another dog lived in the house—her smell was everywhere. Nate carried me inside, and we went straight into a room where I met Hannah. She was just as sweet as Nate. I think it was late, so we all went to sleep pretty quickly.

I must have been exhausted because I slept straight through the night. When I woke up, Hannah and Nate were gone! I listened carefully, and I heard movement downstairs, so I tried to force my way out of the bedroom. The door was shut tight; it was no use. I kept scratching. I was worried I was wrong about Hannah and Nate.

What if they were going to keep me locked up, too?

Luckily, my fears were wrong. Not long after I started scratching, I heard footsteps approaching. Hannah opened the door, and I bolted to escape that room. The steps were the first thing I saw, so I ran down the steps. I met Ben and Lucy for the first time. I ran up and gave them lots of kisses because I was so happy to meet more nice people and to be out of that room. I was so engrossed in my kisses that I didn't notice the smell approaching, but I heard the bark.

I turned to see a brand new kind of dog. She was smaller than me, but not by much. Her face was even flatter than mine, and she had floppy ears. Her tail was fantastic; it was fluffy and curled up in a circle. She seemed friendly, but it was hard to gauge from her small face. She walked up to me slowly and cautiously.

She sniffed me and decided I was a friend. We played our first game–she tried to bite my legs while I tried to bite her ears. Neither of us was successful, but we were both happy to have a friend, or rather, a sister.

The next weeks were a big change for me. I had to learn how to live with my new family. I wasn't used to going outside at all, let alone going outside every time I had to go to the bathroom. It was so cold for a while; I never wanted to go outside if I could help it. I wasn't used to having toys, so I had a bad habit of hoarding or hiding them. I didn't mean to do it; it just happened. I had to learn to avoid Zelda's sneezes. When she wakes up, goes outside, moves, licks—really all the time—Zelda sneezes, and I never wanted to be in her sneeze path.

As the days and weeks passed, I learned the ways of the house. Zelda was great at teaching me how to go on walks and be outside and be a good dog. She also taught me how to avoid getting in trouble for doing something wrong— give lots of kisses and sad Peach eyes.

The best part about living with Zelda is that life is never boring. We always find something to do, a new mystery to solve, or an adventure outside. I love my new home and having a sister, even if she is the star of the series. And one of these days, we will catch a squirrel!

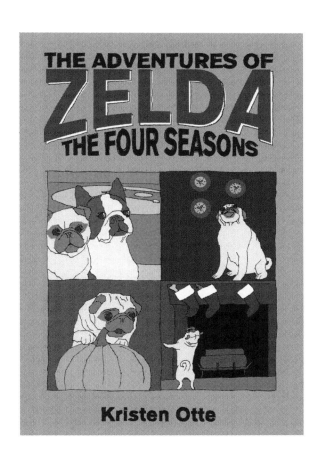

Zelda and Peach's Adventures continue in the fourth book. Available now!

AFTERWORD

Thank you for purchasing this book. If you enjoyed it, please leave a review at Amazon.com or Goodreads. In addition, I invite you to visit my website (kristenotte.com) and join my email list to receive updates on my latest writing projects.

I also want to thank a few people who helped me with this project. First, thanks to my husband for helping me with my writing projects. Not only did he proof this book, but he also helped me capture and edit video interviews with Zelda and Peach. That's love.

Thanks to my family for supporting my writing career and everything I do. A special thanks to my nephew, Alexander, for laughing at Zelda's stories, encouraging me to keep writing.

Thank you to my editor, Candace Johnson, for her hard work and kind words. Thanks to Michael McFarland for designing another awesome cover. And finally, thanks to our pug, Zelda, and our Boston terrier, Peach for allowing me to tell their stories.

ABOUT THE AUTHOR

Author Kristen Otte writes books for children, teens, and adults. Her mission is to bring joy and laughter through stories to people young and old. When she isn't writing or reading, you may find her on the basketball court coaching her high school girls' team. If she isn't writing or coaching, she is probably chasing her husband and dogs around the house.

BOOKS BY KRISTEN OTTE

The Adventures of Zelda: A Pug Tale
The Adventures of Zelda: The Second Saga
The Adventures of Zelda: Pug and Peach
The Adventures of Zelda: The Four Seasons
The Photograph
The Evolution of Lillie Gable

Learn more about Kristen, her books, and her workshops at her website: www.kristenotte.com.

Made in the USA
San Bernardino, CA
15 January 2018